"PRAISE FOR "OTHER" BOOKS

'Will make you laugh out loud, cringe and snigger, all at the same time'
-LoveReading4Kids

'Very funny and cheeky'
-Booktictac, Guardian Online Review

Waterstones Children's Book Prize Shortlistee!

'I LAUGHED SO MUCH, I THOUGHT THAT I WAS GOING TO BURST!'
Finbar, aged 9

'The review of the eight year old boy in our house... "Can I keep it to give to a friend?" Best recommendation you can get' -Observer

'HUGELY ENJOYABLE, SURREAL CHAOS'
-Guardian

I am still not a Loser
WINNER of
The Roald Dahl
FUNNY PRIZE
2013

First published in Great Britain 2015
by Jelly Pie an imprint of Egmont UK Ltd
The Yellow Building, 1 Nicholas Road, London W11 4AN

ISBN 978 1 4052 6913 1

www.futureratboy.com
www.jellypiecentral.co.uk
www.egmont.co.uk

A CIP catalogue record for this title is available from the British Library

Printed and bound in Great Britain by the CPI Group

56628/1

FUTURE RATBOY AND THE ATTACK OF THE KILLER ROBOT GRANNIES

SATURDAY NIGHT IN SHNOZVILLE

Hello, my name is Colin Lamppost and this is the story of how I got zapped millions of years into the future and turned into a superhero rat.

It all started one Saturday night when I was at home in Shnozville, sitting on the sofa with my cuddly toy bird, Bird.

My mum and dad and little sister were on the sofa too, and we were all waiting for . . .

to start on our really old TV.

said my mum, and my dad scrabbled his hand down the side of the sofa, looking for the remote control. He pulled it out and pointed it at the TV.

NOTHING HAPPENED.

'Stupid twiddler!' he grumbled, banging it against his knee, and the volume zoomed up to a hundred.

cried my mum, and my dad got up and plodded over to the telly. 'Blooming telly!' he growled.

TAP!

Suddenly there was a tap on the window. A raindrop had hit the glass and was zigzagging down it like a tear.

'Aw, don't cry, little window!' said my sister, who's one of those sisters who feels sorry for things like windows.

'Hmmm, looks like we've got a problem, Bird,' I said to Bird, even though he was just a cuddly toy bird who didn't understand anything. 'Mr Window's sad, and if we don't cheer him up, my sister's gonna be going on about it all the way through **ATTACK OF THE KILLER ROBOT GRANNIES!**'

Bird's shiny plastic eyes stared at the bowl of popcorn on the table. But only because that was the way he was facing.

I grabbed a tissue, leapt off the sofa and forward-rolled across the living room towards the glass.

'Colin Lamppost to the rescue!' I boomed in my best superhero voice, and I handed the tissue to the window. But because the window didn't have hands, it couldn't take it. 'Argh, foiled again!' I said, crumpling the tissue up in my hand.

Another raindrop tapped against the glass, then about seventeen more. 'Hmmm . . . must be that storm the weatherman was talking about,' I said to Bird.

'Brilliant thinking, Colin!' I squawked, doing Bird's voice for him. 'Thanks, Bird!' I smiled, and I forward-rolled back to the sofa and grabbed a handful of popcorn.

AND THAT WAS WHEN THE BOLT OF LIGHTNING LIT UP THE WHOLE ROOM.

KABOOM!

'WAAAAAHHH!' screamed my sister, and I threw my popcorn in the air, which is something I've always wanted to do.

'Nobody panic!' said my dad, or at least I think it was him, because all I could see was pitch black. The TV had turned off, as well as all the lights in the living room, and everyone else's in the whole street too. 'The lightning must have blown the electrics!' said my dad, and just as he said it, all the lights came back on.

'Phew, that was close!' I said to Bird. 'Thought we might miss ATTACK OF THE KILLER ROBOT GRANNIES for a second there!' I grinned, looking at the TV, which was still black.

cried my mum.

'RIGHT, THAT'S IT!' boomed my dad, pulling the plug out and lifting the TV off its stand.

'I'VE HAD JUST ABOUT ENOUGH OF THIS PIECE OF JUNK!'

he shouted, marching into the hallway and out of the front door, towards our wheelie bin.

'NOOO!' I cried, running out of the living room and diving into the cupboard under the stairs. I grabbed my anorak and put it on, pulling up the hood.

Hanging on a hook was an old scratched-up scuba-diving mask. I'd need that too, what with all the rain outside. 'Operation Save The TV!' I shouted, heading for the front door with Bird tucked underneath my arm.

DISASTER STRIKES

'COLIN SWEETIE, COME BACK HERE!' shouted my mum, as I stretched the scuba mask over my head and zoomed out of the front door, past my dad who was coming back in, minus the TV.

'I'VE GOT TO SAVE THE TELLY!' I shouted. 'OTHERWISE I'LL NEVER SEE ATTACK OF THE KILLER ROBOT GRANNIES!'

A bolt of lightning hit the little apple tree in our front garden and a branch exploded, spraying tiny little bits of bark through the air.

'WAAAAAHHH! BE CAREFUL, MY DARLING!' screamed my mum, as I lifted the lid of our green plastic wheelie bin and dived into it, which is another thing I've always wanted to do.

'Phew, that was close!' I whispered, giving Bird a stroke and patting the TV. My eyes were getting used to the pitch blackness, and I noticed I was sitting on a half-filled-up bin bag, which was actually quite comfy.

'Squeak!' squeaked something, and seeing as it couldn't have been Bird, because he was just a cuddly toy bird that couldn't speak, I looked around the bin for something else that might have made the noise. AND THAT WAS WHEN I SPOTTED THE RAT.

'RAAAAAT!' I screamed. Not that anyone could hear me, what with the lightning bolt hitting the bin.

MILLIONS OF YEARS LATER

I woke up and didn't know where I was. Then I remembered I was in a bin.

I lifted the lid and jumped out. It was morning and the little apple tree in my front garden was now a gigantic, ancient one. 'Coooool!' I said, and I looked up at my house, which was two times taller and more metal-looking than I remembered. 'Also coooool!' I smiled. I like saying 'cool', in case you haven't noticed.

'Mu-um! I'm ho-ome!' I shouted, knocking on the front door.

The door whooshed open like one of the ones at my local supermarket, and an old lady with a shiny metal head and red traffic-light eyes peered down at me. 'HELLO DEAR,' she bleeped, in a robotic voice.

'Hmmm . . . you're not my mum,' I said, scratching my chin and looking her up and down. She had skinny metal legs, just like a robot would, except at the end of them were clippy-cloppy brown shoes. Dented into her metal skirt in scary-looking capitals was the name 'MAVIS 3000'.

CORRECT

bleeped MAVIS 3000, her mouth not moving.

'So where are my mum and dad and little sister?' I said, peering past her into the hallway. Usually our hallway is filled up with trainers and coats and tennis balls and things like that. Now it was just an empty metal tube with flashing buttons on the walls.

MAVIS 3000 opened a little door on her square, metal belly and stuck her claw-hand in, pulling out a mug. 'NICE CUP OF TEA?' she bleeped, pouring a sip's worth into her non-closing mouth. 'MMM,' she pinged, like my mum's microwave, and a cloud of tea steam hissed out of her nostrils and into my face.

'DIVE FOR COVER!' I shouted in my superhero voice, not diving for cover at all. My scuba mask had misted up from all the tea steam, and I backed away down the path, bumping into the green plastic wheelie bin I'd just jumped out of.

Bird fluttered out of the bin. 'WAAAHHH!' he screeched, peering up at MAVIS 3000, and he flew through the air towards me and tucked himself under my arm.

I glanced down at Bird, forgetting about the crazy robot granny for a millisecond, and wiped the tea steam off my scuba mask.

'Something weird's going on here,' I mumbled, poking Bird's fat furry belly, and he squawked. 'Bird doesn't ruffle his fur . . . or fly through the air . . . or squawk when you poke his belly!'

I peered into Bird's shiny plastic eyes, and they blinked. 'YOU'RE NOT BIRD!' I shouted.

NOT BIRD!

screeched Bird, copying what I'd just said, and I was just about to pinch myself to see if I was dreaming, when I heard MAVIS 3000 clip-clopping down the path towards me.

'FANCY A BISCUIT?' she bleeped, towering above us like a lamppost, which is my second name in case you forgot. A chocolate digestive whirred out of a slot in her belly and she pincered it with her claw and slid it into her mouth. 'YUMMY,' she bleeped, and a crunching sound blurted out of the little speaker on her chest.

You know when you chomp on a chocolate digestive and the crumbs start flying out of your mouth? That's what was happening now. Except that the crumbs flying out of MAVIS 3000's mouth were zooming towards my face like billions of tiny bullets.

'ARRGGHH!' screamed a flower sticking out of the front lawn, as a crumb shot through one of its petals. Which was weird, because I'd never heard a flower scream before.

'OOF!' groaned a snail, its shell exploding from a biscuity bullet.

'Operation Don't Get Hit By A Chocolate Digestive Crumb!' I cried, diving into the wheelie bin with Not Bird. My house was on a hilly road, and I'd always wondered what it'd be like to roll down it – NOW WAS MY CHANCE!

'Let's get the uncoolness out of here!' I screamed, as the bin began to move and we zoomed down the slope towards Shnozville High Street.

CLUNK!

The bin crashed to a stop and I crawled out. We'd bumped into a pair of legs with yellow trainers on the end of them. The trainers hovered a centimetre off the pavement, which was lucky, because underneath them was a worm going for his morning stroll.

'Hey, your bin just crashed into my legs!' shouted the owner of the legs, who was an angry-looking lady with a see-through TV screen floating in front of her face. She wasn't actually even looking at me, she was more staring at her screen.

'Good morning! It's Sunkeels the two-hundred-and-seventeenth of Plurgtember, Eight Million and Twelve, and this is today's news...' said the man on the screen.

'Sunkeels?' I said, looking around at Shnozville High Street.

The buildings were about a hundred and seventeen times taller and shinier than I remembered, and the cars floated more than usual. 'What's a Sunkeels?' I said. 'And what was all that about it being Eight Million and Twelve?'

The lady looked down at me, her eyes turning from angry to scared.

'RAAAT!' she screamed, which was weird seeing as I was Colin Lamppost, not a rat, and she zoomed off in her hover-trainers.

Not Bird floated out of the bin and landed on the pavement. 'Not Bird, there seems to be a problem,' I said in my superhero voice. 'I think we might've been zapped into the future!' I cried, pointing around at how shiny and futuristic Shnozville High Street had become.

'NOT!' chirped Not Bird, pecking at a dried-up blob of pink bubblegum, and the blob twitched, slithering off to find a quieter bit of pavement.

'You see!' I said, pointing at the blob. 'You'd never get a bit of bubblegum doing something like that in the old days!'

Not Bird looked up at me and tilted his eyebrows into their scared positions.

'Don't be scared, Not Bird! Colin Lamppost will protect you from the Attack of the Evil Bubblegum Blob!'

I said.

Then I realised he was looking at whatever was behind me.

DOREEN XL97-220

'HELLO DEAR,' bleeped a familiar robotty voice, and I turned round to see MAVIS 3000 standing there with another robot granny.

She was fatter than MAVIS 3000 and had neon-red lipstick zigzagged round her mouth. Dented into her metal skirt in scary-looking capitals was the name 'DOREEN XL97-220'.

Both the robot grannies were carrying handbags and pulling old granny shopping trollies, except unlike normal old granny shopping trollies, these ones floated - probably because we were in the future.

'EEK!' squeaked Not Bird's bubblegum blob, trying to slither off a tiny bit faster, and MAVIS 3000 stomped her foot down on the pavement, spiking it to death with her clippy-cloppy heel. She held her shoe up to DOREEN XL97-220's mouth and waggled her metal eyebrows.

'OOH. TA VERY MUCH, MAVIS,' bleeped DOREEN XL97-220, pincering the blob off MAVIS 3000's heel with her jaggedy metal teeth and starting to chew.

'Operation Back Away Quietly,' I whispered to Not Bird, dragging the wheelie bin in front of us like a smelly plastic shield, and the bin scraped along the pavement, not being quiet at all.

MAVIS 3000 nodded at me with her square head, and her red traffic-light eyes flashed. 'THIS IS THE ONE I TOLD YOU ABOUT, DOREEN,' she bleeped, and DOREEN XL97-220 did a computery-sounding tut.

'OOH, YOU'RE RIGHT, MAVIS. HE IS A BIT RATTY, ISN'T HE?' she bleeped, and I wondered if they maybe weren't talking about me at all, seeing as I wasn't ratty in the slightest, I was Colin Lamppost-y.

I twizzled my head around, looking for that rat that'd been in the bin with me and Not Bird the night before. 'Operation I Reckon It Must Be That Rat They're Talking About, Not Me . . .' I said.

AND THAT'S WHEN I SAW MY REFLECTION IN THE WINDOW OF A PARKED HOVER-CAR.

GASP!

That was how big my gasp was when I saw my reflection.

'RAT!' I shouted, pointing at myself. I pushed my scuba mask on to my forehead and stared at my new reflection.

My nose had whiskers on it and a black blob at the end like a shiny full stop. A pair of aerials poked out of my head, and a plug sat at the end of a cord that was sticking out of my bum. A bin bag hung flappily down my back like a cape, and on my belly fizzled a TV screen.

No wonder that angry-looking woman had screamed when she saw me! Not only had the bolt of lightning zapped me and Not Bird into the future, it'd fused me together with the rat - and my rubbish old TV too!

'WHAT DO YOU RECKON, DOREEN?' bleeped MAVIS 3000. 'NICE SLICE OF RATBOY ON TOAST FOR BREAKFAST?' she said, her shiny metal teeth glinting in the Sunkeels morning sun.

'OOH, I COULD JUST MURDER ONE!' nodded DOREEN XL97-220, pressing a button on the side of her head.

The bubblegum blob she'd been chewing on started to balloon out of her mouth, blowing up to the size of a baby elephant. She crunched her lips shut and the balloon floated into the air, bouncing on the pavement towards my shiny full-stop nose.

'I am NOT a ratboy, my name is Colin Lamppost!' I shouted, as the balloon tried to swallow me whole.

'RATBOY! RATBOY! RATBOY!' squawked Not Bird, and I tucked him under my arm, twizzled round and forward-rolled into the bin, which immediately started to roll away, thank coolness.

'Operation Don't Get Swallowed Whole By A Bubblegum Balloon!' I cried, zooming down the High Street inside my wheelie bin. I leaned left and we skidded down an alleyway, crashing into a wall.

The bubblegum balloon floated past the end of the alleyway, followed by MAVIS 3000 and DOREEN XL97-220, and I breathed a sigh of relief.

'It's just like ATTACK OF THE KILLER ROBOT GRANNIES!' I said, crawling out of the wheelie bin and giving Not Bird a thumbs up.

'NOT!' squawked Not Bird, giving me a thumbs down with the thumb bit of his wing.

AND THAT WAS WHEN I HEARD THE BUZZING NOISE.

I looked up and peered at a man with thirteen eyes.

DINDLE FROGSHNOFF

'No need to be scared, little ratboy!' smiled the man with thirteen eyes. Not that he was a man exactly, he was more of a man-sized fly.

His arms and legs had hairy spikes sticking out all over them, and on his back, neatly folded up like a see-through tablecloth, hung a giant pair of wings. Next to him was a woman-sized fly and two kid-sized ones.

'My name isn't Ratboy, it's Colin Lamppost!' I said, and the man-sized fly chuckled.

'Very nice to meet you, Colin! My name is Dindle Frogshnoff, and I think I might be able to help you,' he buzzed, shooting his hairy hand out to shake.

So I shook it.

Even though it was pretty scary looking.

But not as scary looking as a robot granny claw.

THREE HOURS LATER...

'... and that's how I ended up standing here talking to you!' I said three hours later, once I'd told the Frogshnoff family my whole story.

'Fascinating,' yawned Dindle. 'Now, as I said three hours ago, I think I might be able to help you – I was an orphan once too, you see ...' he buzzed, and my plug-tail twitched.

'Hang on a millisecond, I'm not an orphan!' I said, smoothing my nose-whiskers down with my tongue. 'We're just stuck here for a bit until we work out how to get home, isn't that right, Not Bird?'

'NOT!' screeched Not Bird.

Mrs Frogshnoff patted me on my aerials and grabbed Not Bird, giving him a little cuddle. 'NOT!' he screeched again, wriggling out of the cuddle and lowering himself down on my head like a wig.

'I understand, Colin,' buzzed Dindle. 'But until you DO get home, you'll need a place to rest your head,' he smiled, looking at Not Bird, who'd dozed off and was snoring NOTs.

He pointed up the street to a tall brown building with a shop at the bottom of it called 'Bunny Deli'. On its roof sat a gigantic plastic cheeseburger and chips. Next to them stood an enormous blue cup with a stripy red-and-white straw sticking out of it.

The cheeseburger looked like it'd been designed on a computer. Its bun was all jaggedy like the pixels on a screen, and the chips were zigzaggedy instead of straight like I was used to.

My TV belly rumbled, and I patted it, realising I hadn't had anything to eat in millions of years.

'Lets go see if there's any room at my old orphanage!' grinned Dindle, flapping his wings and buzzing off towards the giant cheeseburger.

I shouted, running after him.

BUNNY
DELI

"BUNNY DELI"

I followed the Frogshnoff family up the street, wheeling my bin behind me. 'Don't worry Not Bird, I'll find a way to get us home!' I said to Not Bird, who'd woken up from his nap and was fluttering next to me.

'NOT!' he squawked, dodging a lamppost, which is my second name, in case you'd forgotten.

'Dindle!' smiled a fat lady standing outside the tall brown building. She was quite a bit older than my mum, and had ten arms. Her hair looked like it was made out of an enormous smelly green mop, and her nose was all pointy like a beak.

Apart from that, she seemed quite nice.

'Bunny!' buzzed Dindle, and I guessed her name must be Bunny.

'Ooh, it's good to see you, Dindle!' grinned Bunny, hugging Dindle with her ten arms, and his thirteen eyes bulged out of their hairy sockets.

'And who do we have here?' she said, peering down at me.

Dindle explained how I'd been zapped into the future and turned into a half rat, half boy, half TV.

'My name's Colin Lamppost,' I said. 'And this is my sidekick, Not Bird.'

'RATBOY! RATBOY!' squawked Not Bird, pointing his beak at me, and I nudged him away while staring through the window of Bunny Deli. Inside were three weird-looking kids, sitting at a table, chatting and laughing.

One of them was a boy with two faces. He was wearing a shiny red suit with two little wings sticking out of the hood. Covering the top half of his two faces were two masks, one for each set of eyes.

Next to him sat an alien with a big bald blue head. His eyeballs were black, and he had pointy, dinosaurish teeth.

The third kid was a girl with round glasses and five arms - two on each side and one in the middle. She was wearing one of those long white coats scientists wear, except with five arm-sleeves instead of the usual two.

Bunny put two of her hands on her hips and scratched her head with the third one. She itched her bum with her fourth hand, and shook hands with Mrs Frogshnoff with number five. Hand numbers six, seven and eight gave the Frogshnoff kids a hug, and she patted me on the head with number nine.

'Well, you look like a lovely little Ratboy to me!' she said, grabbing one of my hands with her tenth one, and she led me into Bunny Deli.

SPLORG AND THE GANG

The Frogshnoff family waved goodbye through the window as Bunny sat me down at the weird-looking kids' table. 'Meet the gang!' she smiled. 'This is Twoface, Splorg and Jamjar,' she said, pointing at the two-faced kid, then the blue alien, then the girl with five arms.

Bunny explained to them how me and Not Bird had been zapped into the future inside a bin.

'There's a spare bed for you upstairs, Ratboy – until we work out how to get you home, of course!' she added, and I nodded, feeling all relieved that Bunny was going to get me home.

Not Bird fluttered across the table and landed on Twoface's hood, right between his two little wings.

'Er, is it just me, or did that bird thing just land on my head?' said Twoface with one of his mouths. 'Hey, I felt that too!' he said with his other mouth, and his wings waggled.

Not Bird squawked and jumped on to the table.

'Don't be rude to our guests, Twoface!' drawled Splorg, who sounded a bit like a slug, if slugs could talk. He picked up Not Bird up and lowered him on to his big bald blue head. 'Nice to meet you, Ratboy!' he said, sticking his hand out all slowly, and I shook it, even though Ratboy isn't really my name.

A see-through floating menu fizzled up in front of my face, and I peered at it, remembering how hungry I was.

'Hello, my name is Malcolm and I'll be your Smellnu today!' said the menu, which was all photos of food, with none of the boring writing bits.

‘What’s a Smellnu?’ I said, and Jamjar pushed her glasses up her nose.

‘It’s a menu you can smell!’ she smiled, waving all five of her arms around. ‘I invented it myself! It was nothing really, just had to bump up the biometrics on the nostrilisation variables. Once that was done, it was simply a matter of decalibrating the choosification modules . . .’

'Gotcha,' I said, my eyes going all blurry, and Bunny put one of her ten arms around Jamjar.

'Jamjar here's my niece,' she said. 'Her mum and dad are famous scientists! Except they accidentally shrunk themselves to the size of full stops during an experiment last year, and nobody can find them anywhere. So Jamjar's staying with us for a bit, aren't you, Jamjar?' she said, and Jamjar nodded, looking a tiny bit sad.

'So . . . your name's Jamjar?' I said, because I'd never met anyone named after a jam jar before.

'Yes, Jamjar!' said Jamjar.

'Nice to meet you, Jamjar!' I said, holding my hand up, and Jamjar high-fived it with one of hers.

I focused my eyes on the Smellnu and noticed that my full-stop nose was a millimetre away from a photo of a cheeseburger. 'Hmmm . . . let's see if this thing really works . . .' I said, breathing in. 'Mmmm, cheeseburger!' I cried, the smell of cheeseburger going up my hairy, ratty nose, and Jamjar tapped the photo with one of her twenty-five fingers.

'You have chosen the Cheesebleurgher Meal Deal!' crackled Malcolm, and the floating see-through Smellnu started to quiver.

A beam of light shot out of the photo, and a computery-looking cheeseburger with zigzaggedy chips fizzled to life on the table in front of me. A pixellated blue cup with a stripy red-and-white straw appeared next to it, and I remembered the giant plastic meal deal I'd seen on the roof of Bunny Deli.

'CheeseBLEURGHer?' I said, lifting the burger up to my mouth and giving it a chomp.

BLEURGH!

burped the cheesebleurgher, and I realised why the cheesebleurgher was called a cheesebleurgher – because it said BLEURGH every time you chomped it!

'Cool times a millicools!' I smiled, picking up a zigzaggedy chip, and Twoface started to laugh. I turned to him and did my 'WHAT?' face, which is just my normal face, but with slightly raised eyebrows.

'Did you just say the word "COOL"?' he chuckled through his left mouth.

'Er, yeah?' I said, chewing on my cheesebleurgher. 'Cool's my favourite word!' I grinned, putting my hand up for Not Bird to high-five it, but he just ignored me.

Twoface shook his head, both his faces rolling their eyes to themselves. 'We say "KEEL" here in the future!' he said out of his right mouth. 'Yeah, Ratboy! Saying "COOL" is the unkeelest thing ever!' he said again, going back to the mouth he'd started this whole thing with.

Bunny winked at me and gave my aerials a ruffle. 'You'll get the hang of it, Ratboy!' she smiled, and I nodded, not that I reckoned saying 'keel' instead of 'cool' was all that hard a thing to get the hang of.

KEEL

I carried on chomping my cheesebleurgher while Splorg slowly tilted his head downwards and started staring at the plug on the end of my tail. 'What's that for?' he smiled with his jaggedy dinosaur teeth.

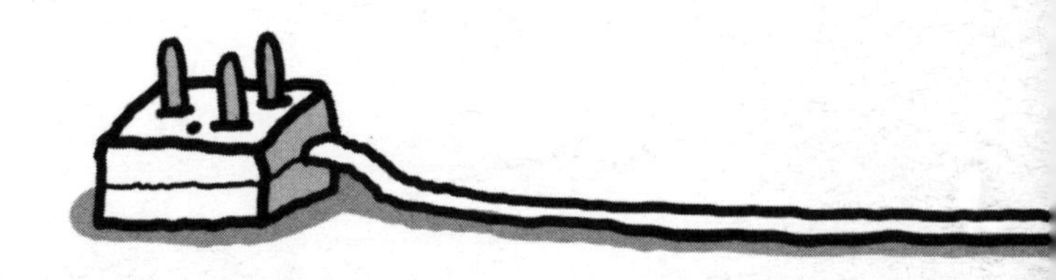

'Excellent question, Splorg!' I said in my superhero voice. Then I said, 'dunno', in my normal voice, seeing as I hadn't really had time to plug my tail in anywhere, what with the killer robot grannies trying to eat me for breakfast and everything.

'Let's see!' blurted Jamjar, pushing her glasses up her nose with one of her hands and grabbing the plug with another.

There was a socket in the wall on the other side of Bunny Deli, far too far away for my tail to reach. 'Here, Socky Socky!' shouted Jamjar, waving her three spare arms, and the plug socket peeled itself off the wall and tiptoed over on two little plug-socket-sized feet.

'KEEL!' I said, saying 'keel' for the first time, which felt keel.

'Good plug socket!' said Jamjar, picking the plug socket up and patting it on its head. 'This is Socky the never-ending plug socket . . . he was my first-ever invention – no wires or anything!' she smiled, plugging my plug-tail into Socky's three little holes, and my bum lifted a centimetre off its seat.

'Keel times a millikeels!' I cried, saying 'keel' for the second and third times, which felt keel times a millikeels, and Bunny patted me on the back all mumsily.

'You're flying, Ratboy! Just like a superhero!' she cooed, and Twoface's two faces screwed into one big fat angry one.

'That's not flying – it's FLOATING!' he scoffed, pointing all four of his eyes at me at once. 'Ratboy's not a superhero. Look at his costume – it's just an anorak with a scuba-diving mask stretched over it, for crying out keel! THIS is a superhero!' he shouted, pointing at himself.

Not Bird ruffled up his fur. 'NOT!' he squawked, giving me a thumbs up with the thumb bit of his wing.

Bunny rubbed Twoface's hood, trying to calm him down. 'Twoface's mum and dad are superheroes too, aren't they, Twoface?' she smiled, picking a bit of fluff off one of his hood-wings, and I wondered why Twoface needed to live in an orphanage if he had a superhero mum and dad.

'Yeah, but it's not as keel as it sounds,' said Twoface, looking up at Bunny while staring down at the table at the same time. 'They're so busy saving the universe, I hardly ever see them . . .' he mumbled.

'That's why Twoface is staying with us for a bit!' Bunny smiled, giving him a cuddle, and he squirmed out of it, even though I could tell he quite liked it.

I thought of my mum and dad and little sister, sitting in our living room, wondering where I was. 'Don't worry Lampposts, I'll be home soon!' I whispered in my superhero voice, and I felt my belly do a rumble.

I glanced down at my tummy, and its TV screen fizzled to life. 'HELP ME!' crackled a bald man with a missing nose, which is a pretty weird thing to see on your stomach.

'Hey, isn't that Dr Smell on Ratboy's belly?' asked Splorg, scraping out of his chair at Splorg-speed and walking over. Jamjar squinted through her glasses at the bald man, and I wondered who in the keelness Dr Smell was.

'ANY-way . . .' I said in my superhero voice, mostly just to change the subject from my belly. 'What are your superpowers, Twoface?'

Jamjar de-squinted her eyes and looked up from my telly belly. 'He can look both ways at once!' she smiled, pointing at Twoface's head. 'What with the two faces and everything . . .' she said, and Twoface did a double-grin.

Not Bird sniggled at how rubbish Twoface's superpowers sounded and I gave him a nudge, holding in a chuckle myself.

'AND I've got sticky hands . . .' said Twoface. 'For climbing up walls and stuff!' he grinned, and he poked one of my zigzaggedy chips with a sticky finger and lifted it out of its packet, popping it into one of his mouths.

Which I had to admit was pretty keel.

'Keel to meet a real life superhero!' I said, scraping out of my chair and holding out my hand, and Twoface shook it with his sticky one.

DR SMELL

Bunny Deli's doors whooshed open and a familiar-looking man staggered in. The main reason he was familiar-looking was that he was the bald one with the missing nose I'd just seen on my telly belly.

'My nose! Somebody's stolen my nose!' cried the man, who was wearing a shiny silver suit. A hover-tie floated in front of his glow-in-the dark pink shirt, and I made a note inside my brain to buy my dad one for a present before I went home.

'Dr Smell!' shrieked Bunny, rushing over to the man, and I thought how weird it was to be called Dr Smell when you haven't got a nose. 'What in the name of Shnozville happened to you?'

Splorg lolloped over to me and cupped his hand round my ear. 'Dr Smell owns the perfume shop down the road. He makes the keelest perfume in the whole of Shnozville – it's Bunny's favourite!' he whispered, moving his cupped hand up and down to keep it where my ear was, seeing as my tail was still plugged into Socky and I was floating around like a balloon.

Dr Smell took a deep breath, but not through his nose, because it was missing.

'It was the weirdest thing,' he said, starting to tell Bunny his story. 'There I was in my shop making a new batch of perfume when I heard a clip-clopping noise,' he warbled. 'I turned round, and blow me down with a feather if I wasn't face to face with a pair of robot grannies!'

He lowered himself down on to a chair and nicked one of my zigzaggedy chips.

I thought back to earlier that day and did a mini superhero gasp. 'Hey, me and Not Bird were chased by two killer robot grannies just this morning!' I said, and Twoface rolled all of his eyes.

'Don't be ridikeelous, Ratboy!' he said, and his other face nodded. 'Yeah Ratboy, nobody comes face to face with a killer robot granny and lives to tell the tale!' he scoffed, even though Dr Smell was right in the middle of telling HIS tale.

Dr Smell gave Twoface the look a man with no nose gives someone when they're ruining his story. 'Anyway, where was I . . .' he said, stealing another chip. 'Ah yes, one of the robot grannies pulled a crumpled-up tissue out of her sleeve and waggled it under my nostrils. Now, it must have had some kind of sleeping potion on it, because the next thing I knew, I'd woken up and my nose had disappeared!' he cried, peering down with cross-eyes at his missing nose.

I looked over Not Bird and mouthed the words, 'MAVIS 3000'.

'NOT!' mouthed Not Bird with his beak, which isn't an easy thing to do, seeing as a beak isn't really a mouth, it's a beak.

'Oh, Bunny, how will I ever be able to make your perfume without my precious hooter?' sobbed Dr Smell, flopping off his chair on to the floor. Bunny whipped a soggy old flannel out of her apron pocket and patted it on his forehead.

'Ooh, those robot grannies, they give me the willies!' she said, and I looked at Not Bird and giggled, because Bunny had just said 'willies'.

'Killer robot grannies are nothing to giggle about, Ratboy,' said Jamjar, looking serious, and I stopped giggling and did my superhero face.

Splorg turned to Twoface, waiting to hear what he had to say, seeing as he was the real superhero out of all of us.

'Sounds like something Mr X might be mixed up in . . .' muttered Twoface, tilting all four of his eyebrows into their serious positions, and I tilted my eyebrows to their pretending-I-am-listening-to-Twoface positions.

Twoface's other face nodded. 'Good thinking, Twoface,' he said, patting himself on the back, and I wondered who in the keelness Mr X could be.

So I asked.

'Er, who's Mr X?' I said, and everybody went quiet.

MR X

'Mr X is the evilest man in the whole of Shnozville,' boomed Twoface with both his mouths at once.

Jamjar took her glasses off and cleaned them on her scientist's coat. 'He was an orphan too, once – when he was a boy like you,' she said, pointing at me with all twenty-five of her fingers.

I AM NOT AN ORPHAN!

I shouted, and Not Bird squawked.

Jamjar raised one of her eyebrows, then carried on talking. 'The only difference is, Mr X didn't have someone nice like Bunny to look after him - HIS Bunny was a mean old lady, isn't that right, Twoface?' she said, but Twoface just ignored her.

He was pacing up and down Bunny Deli, scratching his head, and I wondered if he had two tiny brains inside it, or one normal-sized one.

'This is Mr X,' drawled Splorg, slowly pulling a white plastic cube out of his pocket and holding it up in his blue palm.

'What, he's that little white cube?' I said, peering down, my shiny full-stop nose almost touching it.

'No!' chuckled Splorg, prodding the cube with his finger, and a floating see-through screen popped up. A mean-looking man with a pointy nose wearing a brown cloak rotated on the screen. 'THIS is Mr X,' he said, and I floated over to get a better look.

'Doesn't look very scary to me,' I said, and Not Bird chirped, which I think might've meant he agreed.

Splorg gave the cube another tap, and Mr X shrunk. A giant silver metal scorpion with a V-shaped window for a face appeared next to him, snapping its claws. Its tail curled in the air above its body like an evil question mark and two glowing green eyes stared ahead, blankly. A door on the side of the scorpion slid open and Mr X climbed in and sat down in a chair, scowling through the glass.

'That's Mr X's giant metal scorpion,' said Splorg, his black eyeballs quivering with fear. 'Not that I've ever seen it in real life – mostly he sends his killer robot grannies out to do his dirty work,' he trembled, and the floating see-through screen fizzled into thin air.

'Why's he called Mr X?' I said, peering through the window of Bunny Deli, half expecting a robot granny or a giant silver metal scorpion to come stomping round the corner any second.

Twoface stopped pacing and pointed all four of his eyes at me. 'Because he's very CROSS,' he said.

'Cross?' I said, as Not Bird fluttered through the air and landed on my head.

'Yeah, cross . . . like an "X", get it?' smiled Jamjar, looking down at Dr Smell on the floor where he was still lying.

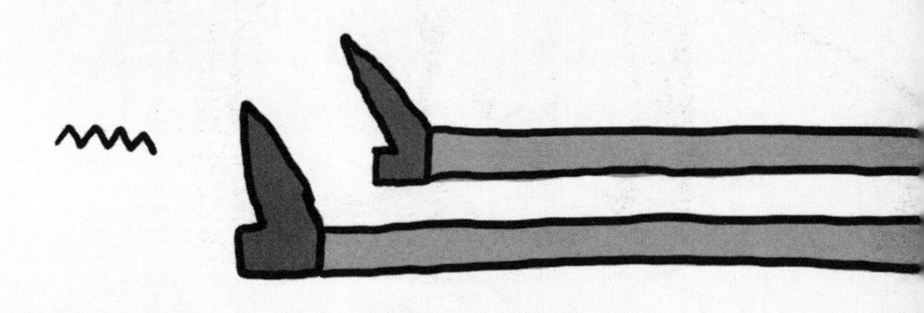

He was doing a sniffing face, except without the twitching-end-of-nose bit, so really it was just a completely still face. 'The weird thing is, I can still smell stuff . . .' he said, as if we were all still listening to his story about how his nose got nicked. 'Like now . . . all I can smell is cheese!' he chuckled, then he started crying again, because having your nose stolen really isn't a laughing matter.

Jamjar whipped a turquoise plastic triangle out of her white coat pocket and started tapping at it with one of her twenty-five fingers.

'What in the unkeelness is that?' I said, wondering how many new things I could see in one day.

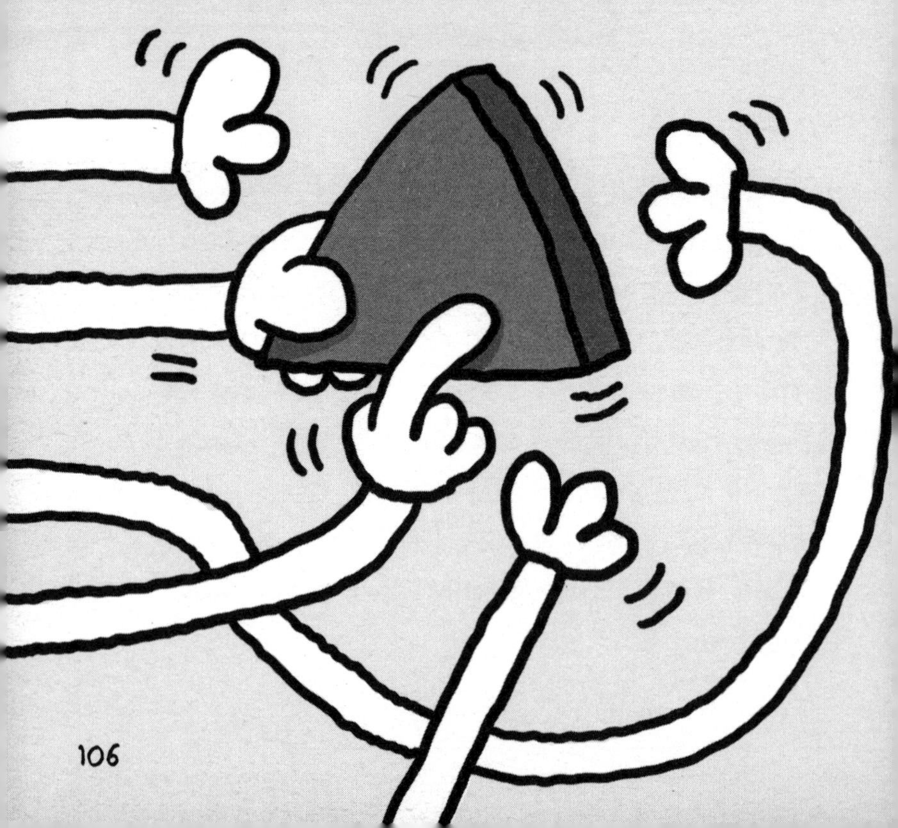

'This?' said Jamjar, flipping the triangle in the air and catching it in another hand. 'This is my Triangulator!' she smiled, and she carried on tapping. 'Very interesting . . .' she muttered, scratching the tip of her nose, and Dr Smell looked at it jealously.

'What's very interesting?' said Splorg.

'Well, according to my Triangulator, there's a ninety-nine point nine, nine, nine, nine, nine, nine percent probability that maybe Dr Smell can smell cheese because his nose has been transportatorised somewhere cheesy . . .' said Jamjar, looking up from her triangle.

I lifted the bun off my half-eaten cheesebleurgher and peered inside, checking to see if Dr Smell's nose was part of my Cheesebleurgher Meal Deal, and Bunny gave me a wink like my mum does when she thinks I'm being sweet.

'Hey, I've had an idea!' said Twoface, clicking his fingers, and we all looked at him. 'Maybe Dr Smell can smell cheese because his nose is somewhere cheesy . . .' he said, and I was just about to say how that was Jamjar's idea when Dr Smell started snoring.

MADE ON THE MOON!

'Is Dr Smell OK?' asked Splorg, and Bunny patted him on his bald blue head.

'He'll be fine, Splorg. Having your nose stolen is a tiring business,' she said, scooping Dr Smell up with all ten of her arms and carrying him over to the see-through lift at the back of the deli.

'Don't mind if Dr Smell lies down in your bed for a while, do you, Ratboy?' she huffed, pressing a button next to the lift, and I gave her a double thumbs up, seeing as I wasn't going to be in the future long enough for it to really be mine.

Bunny and Dr Smell zoomed up in the lift through a hole in the ceiling, and Twoface went back to scratching his head. Jamjar was busy tapping something into her turquoise plastic triangle.

'Hey, I've got an idea!' shouted Splorg, and I jumped, which was the first time I've ever jumped when I was floating off the ground already. 'Maybe Dr Smell's nose is on the moon!' he grinned.

I smiled over at Not Bird, and he sniggled. 'What's so funny about that?' said Splorg, looking all confused.

'Everybody knows the moon's not made out of cheese, Splorg!' I said, flicking the last bite of cheesebleurgher into my mouth and swallowing it whole.

'WRONG!' honked Twoface, double-grinning. 'Don't you know anything, Ratboy?' he said, and before I could say something back, he'd carried on talking. 'I suppose you missed it while you were being zapped here from the year MINUS ZERO, but all the cheese in the world is made on the moon these days!'

I rolled my eyes and did my face I do when I don't believe something.

'It's true, Ratboy . . .' said Jamjar, and then she said the ridikeelest thing I'd ever heard.

'About a million years ago, all the cows on earth started saying "MOON" instead of "MOO". Scientists realised the cows wanted to go to the moon! So they flew them all to the moon! Now all the cows in the whole world live on the moon!'

The lift doors hissed open again and Bunny stepped back out, minus Dr Smell. 'Ratboy doesn't believe all the cheese is made on the moon!' said Splorg, and Bunny sighed, looking all tired like my mum does sometimes.

She wandered over to the fridge and stuck her hand through the door, scrabbling around for something inside. 'Keelness times a millikeels!' I said, because I'd never seen a reach-through-able fridge door before, and Bunny pulled out a wrapped-up rectangle of Cheddar.

'Made on the moon!' said Bunny, holding up the Cheddar for me to see it. The label on it was a photo of a pretty-looking cow, with her name, 'Delores', written underneath.

Delores had very long eyelashes, and earrings in the shape of half-moons hanging off her big, hairy ears. At the bottom of the label, in tiny letters, were the words, 'Made on the Moon'.

Twoface stuck his tongue out and did a raspberry noise with his other mouth. 'Told you, Ratboy!' he grinned, then he snapped his fingers. 'Jamjar! You've got a UFO,' he said. 'Let's fly up to the moon and get Dr Smell's nose back!'

'Whoa, whoa, whoa,' I said, which is something I've always wanted to say. 'Me and Not Bird haven't got time to go to the moon - we've got to work out how to get home!'

Jamjar pulled the Triangulator out of her pocket. She pointed it at my wheelie bin, which had been sitting next to me minding its own business the whole time.

'Hmmm, very interestikeels,' she said, pushing her glasses up her nose. 'Seems like this bin is some kind of portal. Only problem is, its coordinates have been blown. Perhaps if we reversed the polarity on the liddification variables, we could reboot its circuit boards and restabilise the field generators,' she blurbled, and I turned to Splorg, hoping he might know what she was going on about.

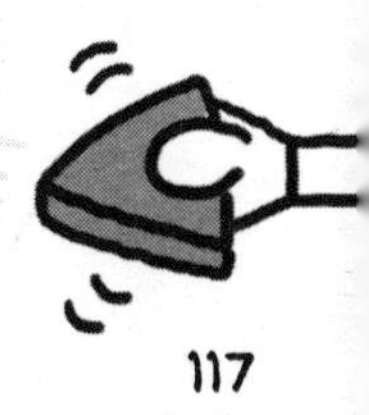

'What she's saying is, the only way you and Not Bird are ever going to get home is if your bin gets zapped by lightning again – with you two inside it, of course!' said Splorg, and Twoface sighed.

'Are we going to the moon or not?' he moaned, stomping his foot, and Jamjar started tapping her Triangulator again.

'Looks like there's a big space storm coming . . . might be a bit blustery,' she said, and then she paused for a millisecond and clicked her fingers.

'Hey!' she cried, looking up at me through her big round glasses. 'We could zap you and Not Bird home with some space-lightning while we're there!'

IN THE BEDROOM

'The UFO's in the bedroom!' said Jamjar, so we all zoomed upstairs in the lift, me floating a centimetre off the floor thanks to my tail still being plugged into Socky.

Dr Smell was lying face-up in my bed, snoring through his mouth. It was the bottom bunk of a bunk bed, and I guessed the top one was Splorg's, because on the wall next to it was a 3D photo of two bald blue-headed aliens.

'Are they your mum and dad?' I said, wondering if it was OK to ask, then realising it was too late because I already had.

'Yeah,' said Splorg, plucking the photo off the wall and sticking his finger into it. The finger poked against his dad's big bald blue head, and it wobbled like a raspberry-flavoured jelly.

'What happened to them?' I said, peering over Splorg's shoulder at the photo. His fat, sweaty dad was wearing a suit and shouting at someone on his phone. His mum was staring into the lens of the camera, pouting her lips like a blue duck.

'Oh, not much. They went out to dinner at some flashy new restaurant right next to a black hole. The black hole swallowed them up whole while they were eating their puddings,' said Splorg all normally, like he was telling a really boring story.

'Sorry to hear that,' I said in my superhero voice, patting Splorg on the shoulder I'd just been peering over, and he shrugged.

'Don't be. They were always going off somewhere, leaving me at home to watch TV on my own,' said Splorg, and I thought how lucky I was that my mum and dad hardly ever went out.

Twoface was on the other side of the room, standing next to his and Jamjar's bunk bed. A pink, scratched-up little UFO, half the size of my mum and dad's car, was standing on the carpet with Jamjar inside it.

'Bagsy sitting in the front!' shouted Twoface, jumping into the passenger seat next to Jamjar, who was fiddling with some flashing buttons and adjusting the rear-view mirror.

Splorg stuck his photo back on the wall and smiled his dinosaur smile. 'Anyway, Bunny took me in after that. She's the keelest – just like a real mum!' he said, and Jamjar and Twoface both nodded.

Bunny ran into the room, huffing and puffing as she handed me a brown paper bag. I peered into it and spotted a donut sitting on top of a pile of other donuts that went on into the distance as far as I could see.

'Just a silly little farewell pressie,' she warbled, giving me a ten-armed cuddle.

'You be careful up there, Ratboy,' she said, peering out of the window at the moon.

Splorg clambered into the back seat of the UFO, and Not Bird fluttered after him, landing on his head.

'Thanks for everything, Bunny,' I said, even though she hadn't done that much apart from be really nice to me. I plonked my bin in the back seat next to Splorg and slid in next to it, making myself as comfortable as possible, which wasn't very.

Jamjar pressed a thumb down on her Triangulator and the bedroom wall lowered like a drawbridge on a castle. 'Ooh, and don't forget to pick me up some Edam!' shouted Bunny, as the UFO hovered off the carpet and we zoomed into the sky.
#

TELLY BELLY

'Everything keel, Not Bird?' drawled Splorg, as we wobbled through space at a millikeels miles per keelness.

'NOT!' squawked Not Bird, who was still on top of Splorg's head, looking like a wig that was about to be sick.

I grabbed a donut out of my brown paper bag and stuffed it into my mouth. 'WAAAHHH!' screamed the donut, as I chomped it up with my teeth and swallowed it whole.

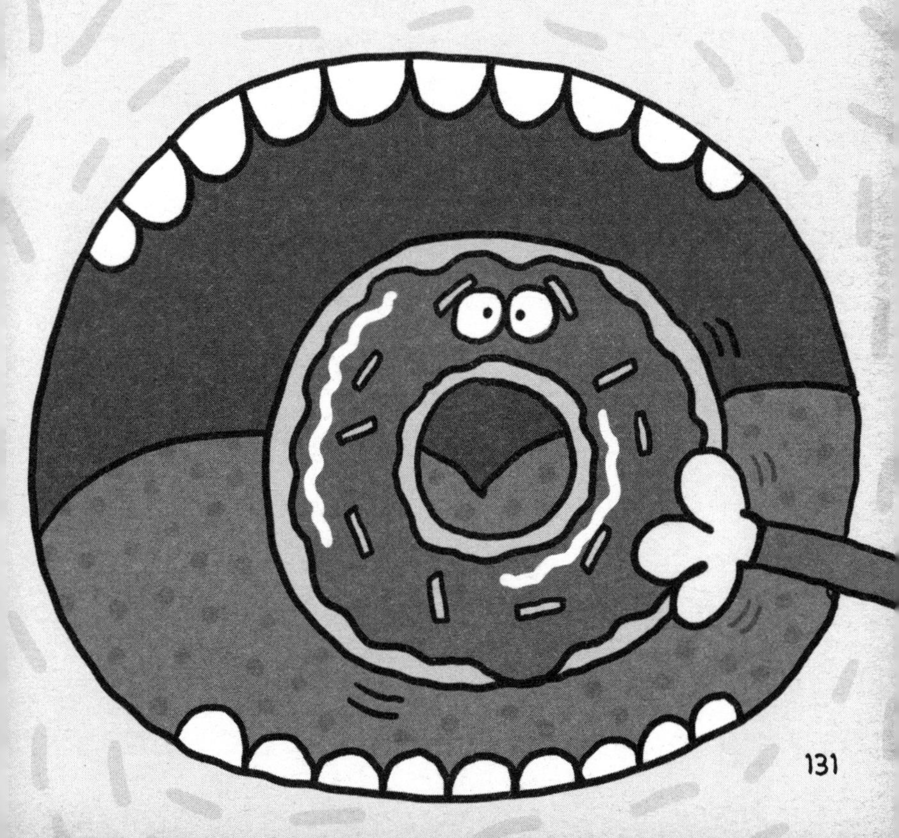

'Mmm, talking donuts!' I smiled, grabbing another one and holding its hole up to my eye like a squidgy telescope. I peered through it and spotted Earth, floating away from us at superkeelness speed. 'Keel times a millikeels!' I gasped, dropping the donut back into the brown paper bag, and it breathed a sigh of relief, even though I was definitely going to eat it later.

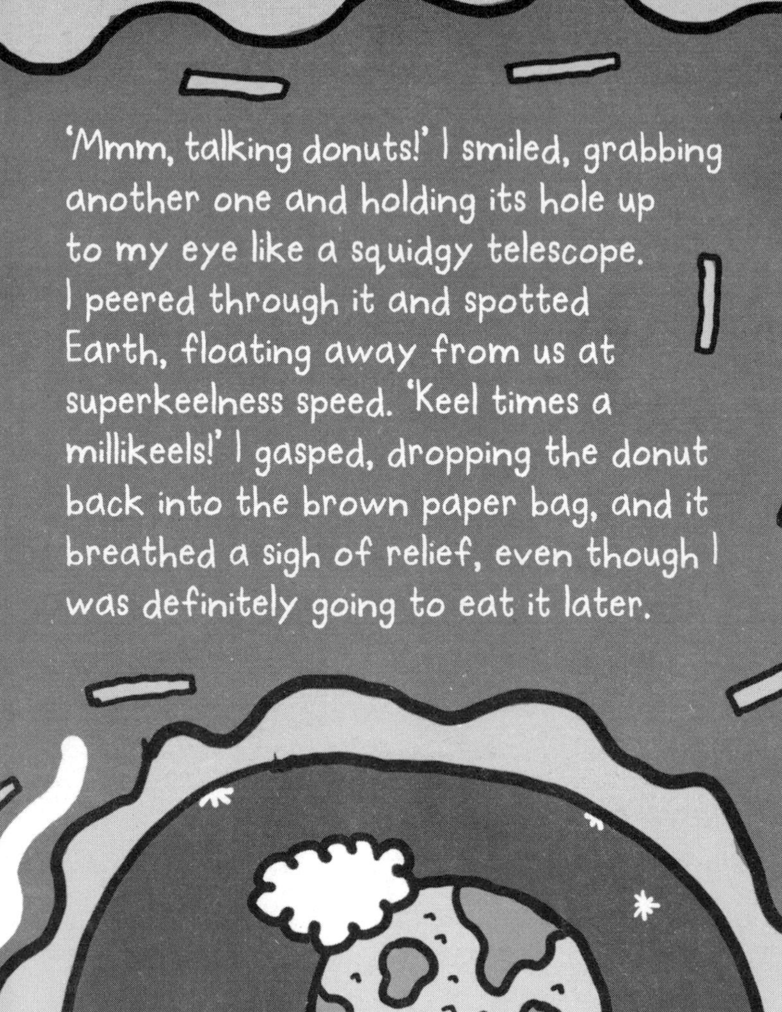

Twoface twizzled one of his faces round from the front seat, bonking Not Bird off of Splorg's head.

'Remember gang, if Dr Smell's nose is on the moon, that means Mr X and the killer robot grannies might be there too,' he said, and Not Bird fluttered over to me for a cuddle, looking a tiny bit scared.

'Don't worry Not Bird, I won't let Mr X and his horrible killer robot grannies stop us from getting home!' I said, my eye swiveling down to look at donut number two again, and the UFO jolted, then swerved, then spluttered.

'We're entering the moon's meteorocheesiological force field!' cried Jamjar, dodging a passing taxi, and the driver waggled his arm out the window. Not that it looked much like an arm. It was more of a leg. With three feet on the end of it. Also, each foot had nineteen toes.

Twoface grabbed the sides of his seat and gritted both sets of teeth as Jamjar spun the steering wheel to the right and prodded about fourteen buttons, all at the same time. 'Firing up the reverse-velocity turbo-thrusters for landing!' she said, and my telly belly started to fizzle.

I looked down and spotted a familiar-looking cow, peering out of the fuzzy screen. 'HELP ME!' mooed Delores the made-on-the-moon-cheese cow. There was something different about her, but I couldn't quite put my finger on what it was.

'Hey, isn't that Delores?' said Splorg, pointing at my telly belly, and the UFO started to shudder.

'Hold on, this is going to be bumpy!' cried Jamjar, as I slotted donut number two into my mouth and we shot through a storm cloud, crash-landing on the moon.

ON THE MOON

I opened my eyes and didn't know where I was. Then I remembered I was in a UFO. On the moon. Which was made out of cheese.

I stuck my head out of the window and looked around. We'd landed on an island of Cheddar, surrounded by a sea of wavy milk. Parmesan flakes circled in the sky like snow, and a couple landed on my hood, making me feel like a bowl of spaghetti Bolognese.

'Argh, my nose!' cried Twoface. 'Argh, my other nose!' he cried again. He was upside-down on top of Jamjar, his bum squidged into her face.

'Everyone OK?' whimpered Splorg from his seat, poking his head over the top of my bin, and Not Bird squawked 'NOT', even though he was fine.

'All keel here!' I said, looking down at my belly for Delores, but she'd disappeared.

There was a hover-bridge in front of us leading to the main part of town, so we all jumped out of the UFO and ran across the bridge to look for her.

An enormous purple cloud rumbled above us like a giant space-monster's duvet. In the distance, a bolt of lightning zigzagged through the sky.

'If this weather keeps up we'll be home in no time!' I said to Not Bird, wheeling my bin behind me.

'NOT!' squawked Not Bird, as a cow drove past us in a Brie-shaped hover-van, heading towards a mahoosive cheese factory in the shape of a slice of Emmental. A floating screen hovered next to the factory, playing cheese adverts at full volume.

'Mooooon cheese is the keelest!' mooed Delores on the screen, her moon earrings swaying, and I tried to work out what'd been so different about her on my telly belly.

I parked my wheelie bin and pulled donut number three out of my brown paper bag. 'OH PLEASE DON'T, MR RATBOY,' it begged, as I held it up to my mouth, and my eyes zoomed in on Delores's ears.

CHEESE FACTORY

'I've got it!' I said, swallowing the donut in one go. 'She didn't have any ears!' I cried, running towards the cheese factory with my bin behind me.

'Where in the unkeelness are we going?' cried Twoface, running after me. Splorg and Jamjar were behind him, also running, even though no one knew what the keelness was going on except for me.

'The cheese factory, of course!' I shouted, Not Bird fluttering next to me like a donut without a hole. 'Delores's ears have been stolen, just like Dr Smell's nose!' I said.

Twoface skidded to a stop, and his two faces stopped nodding. 'Hang on a millikeels, why are we running to the cheese factory then?' he said, and I swiveled my head around.

'Delores MUST work in the cheese factory!' I shouted, hover-jogging backwards, which is something I've always wanted to do. 'All we have to do is find her, then we can catch Mr X and the killer robot grannies that stole her ears - and Dr Smell's nose!' I cried, running out of breath from all the explaining I was doing.

Twoface screwed his two faces up into one big stupid one, trying to work out what was going on. 'I've got it!' he said, clicking his fingers. 'Let's head to the cheese factory and look for Dolores!' he boomed, starting to run towards it, and I looked up at the storm cloud, which was rumbling even more than before.

DWAYNE THE STUPID LOOKING COW

The doors of the giant cheese factory whooshed open and we skidded to a stop in front of the reception desk. 'Welcome to the cheese factory!' mooed a stupid-looking cow with cross-eyes and buck teeth from behind the desk.

Twoface slammed his hand down on the desk and tried to lift it back up, which wasn't easy, what with it being all sticky. 'We need to see Delores!' he boomed, looking left and right at the same time.

'Just one second,' said the cow, pressing a button on his phone with his hoof and smiling at us pleasantly while waiting for an answer.

I smiled back, feeling bad about that Cheesebleurgher Meal Deal I'd eaten earlier. From now on I was going to be a vegetarian, I thought to myself. Then I thought about how tasty the cheesebleurgher had been, and I changed my mind.

'Delores? This is Dwayne from reception,' mooed Dwayne into his phone. 'I've got a boy with two faces, an alien with a big blue bald head, a girl with five arms and and a floating ratboy with a TV on his belly here in reception for you . . .'

Not Bird did a cough and pointed one of his wings at himself. 'NOT!' he squawked, and Dwayne held his hoof up, mouthing 'sorry' for leaving him out. Which isn't easy when you're a cow. Actually, wait a second, yes it is.

'What's that, Delores, you can't hear me because your ears have been stolen?' mooed Dwayne, and Twoface glanced at Jamjar and raised all four of his eyebrows.

DELORES'S OFFICE

'Quick, before the robot grannies escape with Delores's ears and Dr Smell's nose!' shouted Twoface, running over to the lifts and pressing the 'Up' button.

'You can't go up to Delores's office which is on the top floor – you haven't got an appointment!' Dwayne mooed, as we squidged into the lift.

'Thanks for the tip!' grinned Jamjar, pressing the top floor button and waving her four other hands goodbye, and the lift doors whooshed shut in Dwayne's stupid-looking face.

The lift doors whooshed open twelve milliseconds later and we all tumbled out, me doing a hover-forward-roll because of how keel I am.

I glanced through the windows of Delores's office and spotted a bolt of lightning in the distance, streaking across the sky like those blue liney bits you get in Stilton cheese. We'd have to hurry, otherwise I'd miss the storm.

'Operation Get Delores's Ears Back For Her Then Head Outside Before It's Too Late For Me And Not Bird To Get Zapped Home!' I said to Not Bird, as we walked towards Delores.

'WAAAHHH!' moo-screamed Delores, and I could understand why. I'd do a scream too if a boy with two faces, an alien with a big blue bald head, a girl with five arms, a floating ratboy with a TV on his belly and a flying toy bird started walking towards me.

'WHAT DO YOU WANT FROM MEEEE?!' she moo-wailed, holding her hooves up, karate-style.

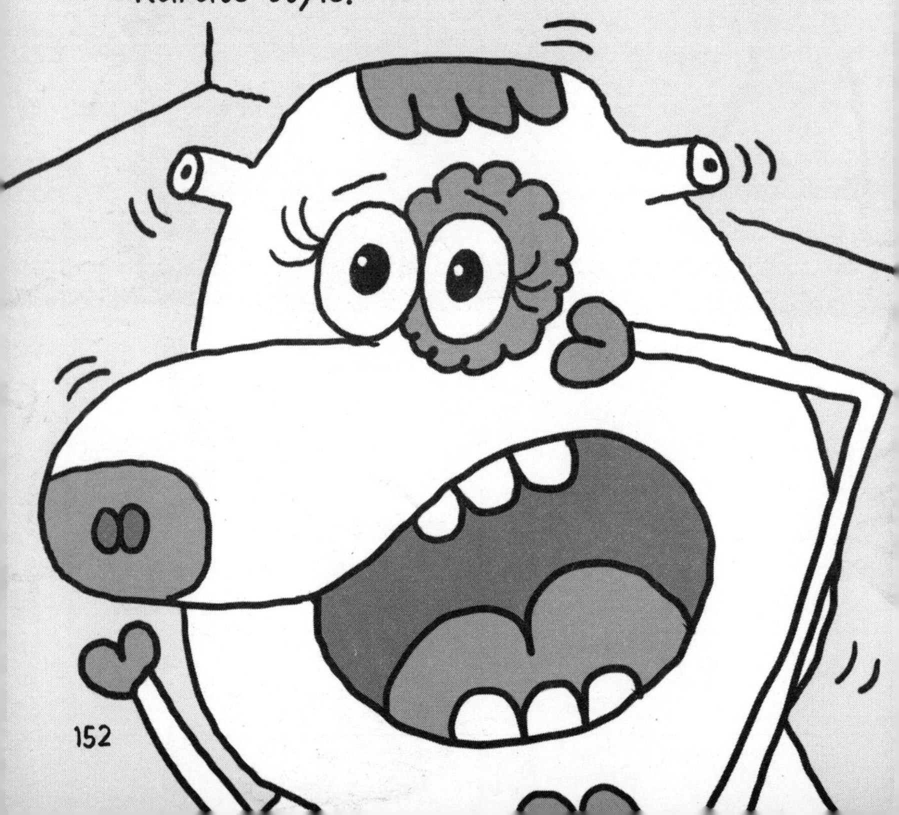

Twoface put his hands on his hips, trying to look all superhero-ish. 'Don't be afraid, Delores, we're here to help!' he said, and she cupped her hooves behind the holes where her ears used to be.

'Pardon?' she mooed. 'I can't hear you. A weird-looking old metal lady carrying a nose under her arm just stole my ears!' she said, and we all looked at each other, which took a lot longer than you'd imagine, seeing as there was quite a lot of us.

Jamjar pulled the Triangulator out of her pocket, pointed it at Delores, and started tapping. 'Hmmm, that's curiokeels,' she said. 'My Triangulator's locator diodes are blocked - must be the storm.'

She looked up at Delores. 'Did the killer robot granny say anything about where she was going next . . . or why she wanted your ears?' she asked, pushing her glasses up her nose for the fifteen billionth time.

'I can't hear you!' mooed Delores, rolling her eyes and fluttering her eyelashes. 'She just took my ears and clip-clopped off. Now all I can hear is this weird buzzing noise,' she mooed, and I felt my tail do a little waggle.

'Buzzing . . .' I muttered to myself, remembering how Dindle Frogshnoff had buzzed quite a lot, what with him being a man-sized fly and everything.

'Maybe the killer robot grannies are going to steal Dindle Frogshnoff's thirteen eyes next!' I gasped.

Twoface leaned his two superhero-ish faces up to my one ratty one. 'Nice idea, Ratboy!' he whispered. 'Yeah Ratboy, mind if I pinch it?' he grinned, and he turned to face the others. 'Guys, I've got an idea!' he boomed, clicking his fingers. 'Maybe the buzzing noise is coming from Dindle Frogshnoff!'

GETTING ZAPPED HOME

'Hey, that was my idea!' I shouted, running into the lift after Twoface and the gang, with my bin trailing behind me. Not that I was all that bothered about him stealing it, seeing as I was about to get zapped home.

The storm was right above us, and we zoomed through the whooshing doors of the cheese factory and back over the bridge on to the island of Cheddar.

Jamjar, Splorg and Twoface jumped into the UFO as I scoffed donut number four, chucking the brown paper bag into my wheelie bin for safe keeping. I climbed into the bin after it and tucked Not Bird under my arm, looking up at the storm cloud.

'Keel to meet you all, good luck with the killer robot grannies!' I grinned, pulling the bin lid over my head, and everything went dark.

'Any second now!' I whispered to Not Bird, thinking back over our adventure, and Not Bird whisper-squawked a 'NOT'. 'Been fun, hasn't it!' I smiled, even though there wasn't any point doing a smile, because Not Bird couldn't see it in all the pitch-blackness.

screeched Not Bird again, and I drummed my fingers against the inside of the bin, wondering what the hold-up was with the lightning.

'Where is it?' I said, reminding myself of my mum when we were waiting for a bus back in the past, and I pushed the lid up a millimetre and peeked out.

Twoface, Jamjar and Splorg were sitting in the UFO, all eight of their eyes looking at me. 'What?' I said, which is what I say when I'm being stared at like that.

WHAT'S HAPPENING?!

I shouted, and I flipped the lid up and stuck my whole head out.

I peered into the sky and spotted the giant purple storm cloud, floating off into the distance. 'My lightning!' I cried, as Splorg jumped out of the UFO and lolloped over.

'Looks like you missed your chance, Ratboy,' he said, putting his arm round my shoulder, and I stared down into my bin at the paper bag of never-ending donuts. Not that I was hungry or anything, I just didn't feel like looking at anyone.

'Me and my stupid plan to go and save Delores!' I mumbled, my voice echoing inside the bin. 'If only I'd kept my mouth shut I'd be home right now watching ATTACK OF THE KILLER ROBOT GRANNIES with my mum and dad and little sister . . .'

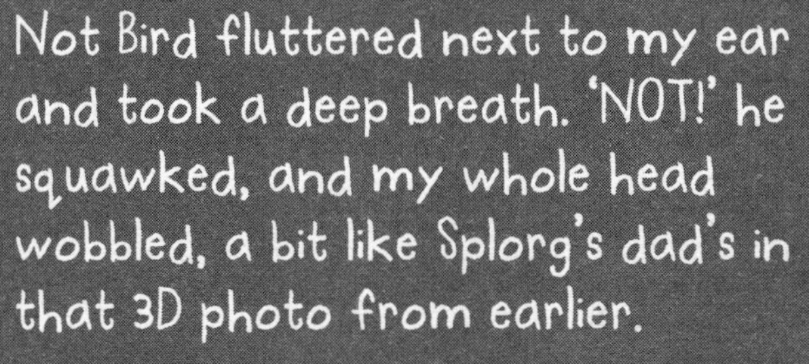

Not Bird fluttered next to my ear and took a deep breath. 'NOT!' he squawked, and my whole head wobbled, a bit like Splorg's dad's in that 3D photo from earlier.

Jamjar jumped out of the UFO and Twoface squidged over into the driver's seat. She pulled the Triangulator out of her pocket and tapped it with a few of her fingers.

'By my calkeelations, the probability of another lightning storm within the immediate proximity of Shnozville's geographical coordinates is medium to high,' she said, as Splorg grabbed the bin's handle and dragged me over to the UFO.

'What do you reckon, Ratboy,' he smiled, nodding at the UFO. 'Fancy a ride back to Shnozville?'

'I spose,' I grumbled, clambering out of the bin and slotting it into the UFO's back seat.

Twoface twizzled his faces round from the driver's seat and smiled. 'If it makes you feel any better, I was looking forward to you getting zapped by lightning!' he chuckled, and I was just about to join in with his chuckle when my telly belly rumbled.

'Ratboy, your stomach!' blurted Splorg, pointing at my belly, and I looked down. Staring out of it was a fuzzy, scared-looking Dindle Frogshnoff.

'HELP ME!' buzzed Dindle Frogshnoff, his thirteen eyebrows all waggling, and I suddenly forgot all about going home, at least for another half an hour or so.

'Operation Save Dindle Frogshnoff!' I boomed, leaping into the UFO with Not Bird under my arm.

BACK TO SHNOZVILLE

'What in the unkeelness do Mr X and the killer robot grannies WANT with all these body parts?' said Jamjar, as Twoface steered the UFO down towards Shnozville nine and three-quarter minutes later, which isn't bad, seeing as we'd flown all the way from the moon.

'First they take Dr Smell's nose, then they steal Delores's ears. Now they're after Dindle Frogshnoff's thirteen eyes!' she cried, as we crashed into a tree.

The UFO slid down a branch and bounced off the end, smashing in half on the pavement like a giant egg.

That sounds a lot worse than it was, by the way.

I climbed out, dragging my wheelie bin with me, and looked up at the sky. It was a beautiful afternoon and the sun was shining.

'Oh my unkeelness!' said Twoface, running across the road. Weirdly and luckeely, we'd crash-landed right in the spot where Dindle Frogshnoff had been attacked by a robot granny.

'Mr Frogshnoff!' I cried, doing one of my mahoosive gasps. Dindle Frogshnoff was lying on the pavement, his tablecloth wings splayed out underneath him. Dotted around on his face, where his thirteen eyes used to be, were thirteen no-eyes.

He sniffed his long, spindly nose in the air and smiled. 'Colin!' he said, recognising me from my smell, and I wondered if I really stank or something. After all, I hadn't changed my pants for millions of years.

'Oh, Colin, it was terrible!' cried Dindle, completely ignoring Twoface, who was standing right next to me. 'Killer . . . robot . . . grannies,' he sobbed, and I thanked keelness he hadn't bored me with some long story about how his eyes had been stolen.

'Did you see which way they went?' I said, looking left and then right, and Twoface's two faces scoffed.

'I'll ask the superhero-ish questions, thank you very much, Ratboy!' he said, looking left and right at the same time, just to show off. 'Did you see which way they went, Mr Frogshnoff?' he smiled, and Dindle rolled his no-eyes.

Jamjar stepped forwards and pulled out her Triangulator. 'I know this sounds stupid, Dindle,' she said, pointing it at him and tapping it with her finger, 'but can you SEE anything inside your head?'

'HUH?'

said Dindle, not really understanding.

'Well . . .' said Jamjar, starting to explain. 'When Dr Smell's nose was stolen, he could actually SMELL where it'd gone. Same with Delores's ears – she could HEAR your wings buzzing!'

Dindle crumpled his face up and curled his nose into a coil, trying his keelest to SEE where his eyes had gone.

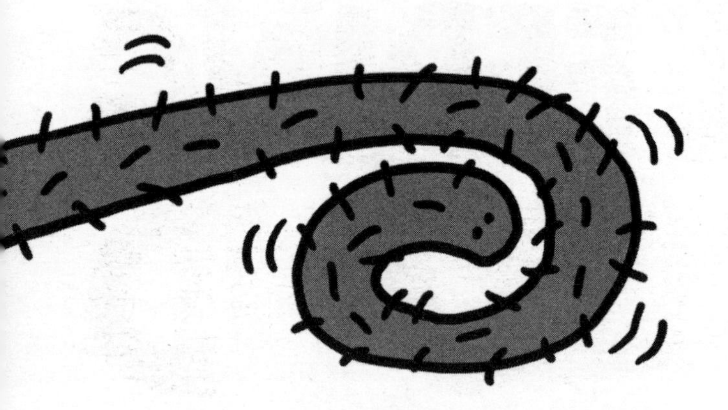

AND THAT WAS WHEN I HEARD THE FAMILIKEELS BLEEPING SOUND.

FAMILIKEEL'S BLEEPING SOUND

'WE MEET AGAIN, MR RATBOY,' bleeped a robotty voice, and I turned round. Standing there were DOREEN XL97-220 and another robot granny with 'PHYLLIS 1200L' stamped into her metal skirt.

Slotted on to PHYLLIS 1200L's face was a huge pair of square glasses, their lenses the same width as Socky.

'NOT!' screeched Not Bird, circling round the robot grannies like a furry little helicopter, and they waved their coily arms, trying to swat him away.

'Killer robot grannies!' cried Splorg, grabbing Not Bird and plonking him on his head. 'Run for it!' he screamed, heading down the road towards Bunny Deli.

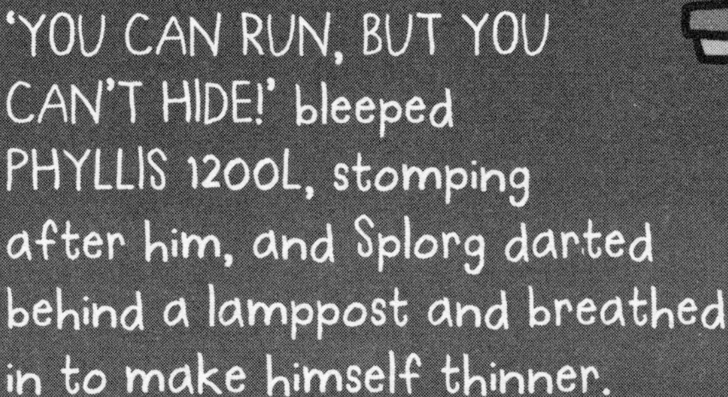
'YOU CAN RUN, BUT YOU CAN'T HIDE!' bleeped PHYLLIS 1200L, stomping after him, and Splorg darted behind a lamppost and breathed in to make himself thinner.

PHYLLIS 1200L stomped straight past the lamppost, completely not seeing Splorg at all, even though his nose was sticking out of one side and his massive blue back-of-head was sticking out of the other. She turned left and stepped into the road, falling down a manhole and smashing to smithereens at the bottom. Which was handy.

Twoface helped Dindle to his feet and we all started running after Splorg, me wheeling my bin behind them. DOREEN XL97-220 was clip-clopping after us in her high-heeled shoes, scrabbling her claw around in her handbag for something to throw at us.

'BUNNY DELI!' croaked Dindle, his nose still in a coil.

'Yes, that's right Mr Frogshnoff, we're going to Bunny Deli,' said Twoface, smiling at Dindle with one of his faces, and a lipstick bonked him on the head.

'BUNNY DELI!' croaked Dindle again, as a comb and one of those little round fold-up mirrors grannies carry around with them flew past his crumpled-up face.

Twoface sighed and sped his running up to superkeelness speed. 'I heard you the first time, Dindle,' he said, looking over at Jamjar. 'I think he might've bumped his head on the pavement or something – he keeps saying "BUNNY DELI"!' he whispered, and I spotted the giant plastic cheesebleurgher, chips and blue cup on top of Bunny Deli coming into view.

DOREEN XL97-220 stopped chasing us and bent over to look at a familikeels little worm. It was familikeels because it was the same one I'd spotted going for a stroll underneath the angry-looking woman's hover-trainers earlier that morning.

The worm was sitting outside a tiny coffee shop, sipping on a cup of coffee and watching the world go by.

'DON'T MIND IF I DO!' bleeped DOREEN XL97-220, pincering the worm with her claw and chomping it in half, and the sky rumbled, as if it was annoyed.

I glanced up in the sky and spotted a giant purple cloud. 'Must be that storm Jamjar was talking about!' I cried to Not Bird, but he was too busy looking at the half a worm that was left in DOREEN XL97-220's claw to take any notice of me.

A worm waiter ran out of the coffee shop, waggling his broom in the air. 'No eating the customers!' he wailed, clearing the chomped-in-half worm's coffee away, and Dindle opened his mouth to speak again, even though we all knew what he was going to say.

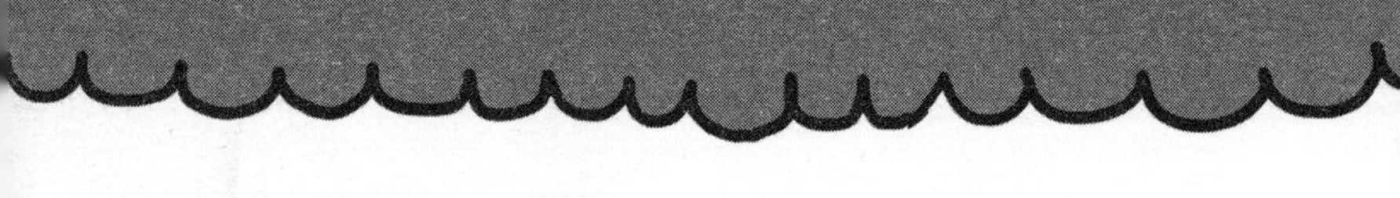

'BUNNY DELI!' he croaked, and Twoface stopped running and put his hands on his hips.

'Would you STOP saying BUNNY DELI!' he boomed, as my telly belly started to fizzle.

BUNNY ON MY TELLY BELLY

I looked down at my telly belly and spotted a scared-looking Bunny, waggling her ten arms.

'BUNNY!' screamed Jamjar, turning to point her Triangulator towards Bunny Deli. 'No wonder Dindle's been saying BUNNY DELI so much – that must be where his eyes are!' she gasped.

Twoface screwed his two faces into one stupid-looking one, trying to work out what was going on. 'I don't get it,' he said. 'Neither do I!' he said again.

Jamjar grabbed Twoface by the shoulders and pushed her glasses up her nose, which is the kind of thing you can only really do if you've got at least three arms.

'Don't you see – if Dindle's eyes are at Bunny Deli, that means the robot granny who's got them is there too!' she said, and Twoface double-gasped. 'And if Bunny is on Ratboy's telly belly, that means she's in big trouble. Maybe a granny is trying to steal her ten arms!' Jamjar cried, running off towards Bunny Deli again.

Twoface scratched one of his noses, and then went to scratch the other one, but changed his mind. 'Hey, I've got it!' he said, clicking his fingers. 'Mr X and the robot grannies are after Bunny's arms!'

OUTSIDE BUNNY DELI

We caught up with Splorg and Not Bird and skidded to a stop on the pavement opposite Bunny Deli, me doing a hover-forward-roll again because of how keel I am.

'Stick with me, gang!' said Twoface, using his two faces to look both ways before crossing the road. 'Good work, Twoface!' he smiled, patting himself on the back, and I spotted a giant metal scorpion, climbing up the side of the building with its giant snappy claws.

'Mr X's giant metal scorpion!' cried Splorg, and a shudder went down my spine and all the way to the end of my tail.

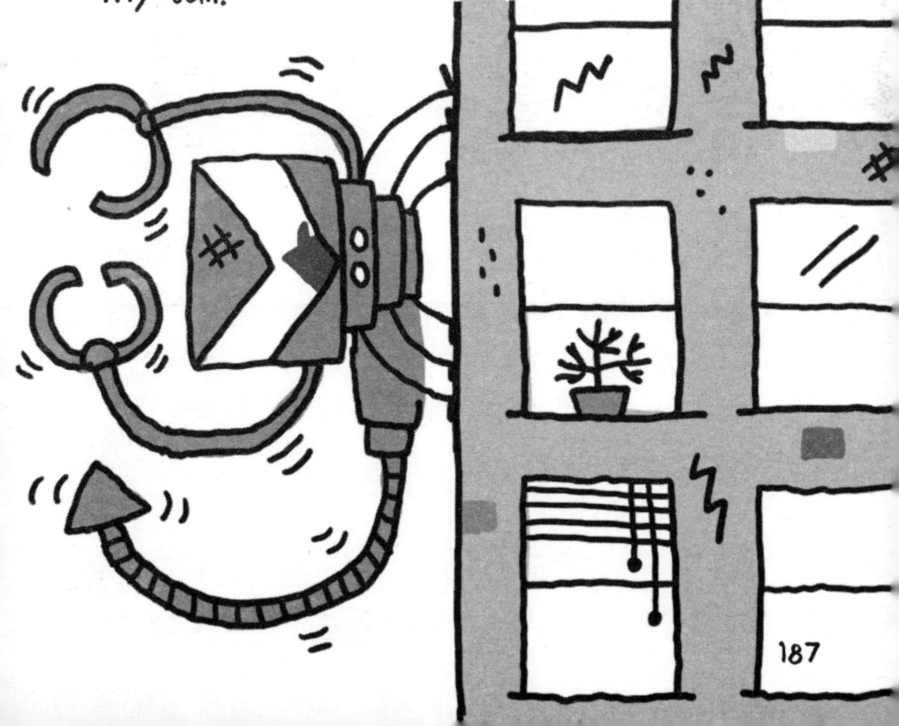

'We've got to stop him!' said Twoface, putting his hands on his hips and staring up at the building, then gasping. 'BUNNY!' he boomed. Bunny was clambering up the fire escape steps away from the metal scorpion, towards the giant plastic cheesebleurgher.

'HELP ME!' she screamed, as thunder clapped in the sky above, and I wondered if the storm thought it was watching a show in a theatre or something, what with it clapping and everything.

'I'm coming, Bunny!' cried Twoface, sticking one of his sticky hands on to the side of the building and starting to climb after the scorpion.

DOREEN XL97-220 appeared behind us, lifting a crumpled-up old tissue out of her purse and throwing it at my head.

'TAKE THAT, RATBOY,' she bleeped, as the tissue bounced off one of my aerials and landed in a puddle.

Splorg and Jamjar ran round to the bottom of the fire escape and started running up it. 'Come on, Ratboy!' shouted Splorg, as I parked my wheelie bin, and looked down at my feet, which were floating a centimetre off the pavement, thanks to Socky.

I plonked Not Bird on my head, grabbed my bin by its handle, and closed my eyes. 'Operation Fly All The Way To The Roof, Save Bunny, Then Get Zapped Home By Lightning!' I boomed, as the sky started to clap again.

MOODY DOG CLOUD

'BY THE POWER OF PLAYING IT KEEL TIMES A MILLIKEELS!' I boomed, feeling my aerials waggle as I zoomed through the air. Then I opened my eyes, looked down again and realised I was only a centimetre off the ground.

Not Bird was still on my head, waggling my aerials with his beak, and DOREEN XL97-220 had clip-clopped over to the fire escape and was blocking anyone else from going up.

'Hmmm, looks like we're gonna have to do this the hard way!' I said, hover-forward-rolling over to DOREEN XL97-220 while trying to come up with another superheroish plan.

'Got it!' I smiled, clicking my fingers and pointing at a little cloud that was gliding by. It was floating above a grumpy-looking dog, who was walking past holding a lead, taking a purple hamster for a walk.

'WHAT'S THAT?!' I cried, and DOREEN XL97-220 turned her head to look. 'Ha, ha, made you look!' I giggled, hover-running between her legs and up the stairs.

'NOT. SO. FAST,' bleeped DOREEN XL97-220, her coily metal arm shooting out of its socket after me.

'NOT!' screeched Not Bird, pecking at her big fat metal bum, not that it did anything.

'WAHHH!' I screamed, as she grabbed me by the tail and flipped me back on to the pavement.

'DON'T MIND IF I DO.' she bleeped, pincering Socky off the end of my tail and slotting him into the side of her head for safe keeping.

'SOCKY!' I cried, even though all he ever did was make me float a centimetre off the ground, and I peered up at the side of the building, just to see how everyone else was doing.

Twoface had reached the roof of the building and was whacking Mr X's giant metal scorpion over the head with one of the giant plastic zigzaggedy chips from the giant plastic Cheesebleurgher Meal Deal.

Splorg and Jamjar were almost at the top, and Bunny had climbed up the massive straw sticking out of the giant blue cup. She was cowering inside the hole at the top of it, looking a tiny weeny bit scared.

'How in the keelness am I gonna get up there now?' I said out loud, even though I was only thinking it. And that was when I spotted Not Bird fluttering into my bin and back out of it, this time with the brown paper bag full of donuts in his beak.

'Thanks, Not Bird, but I'm not really hungry right now,' I said, thinking what a rubbish sidekick he could be sometimes, and the sky clapped, this time with some lightning too.

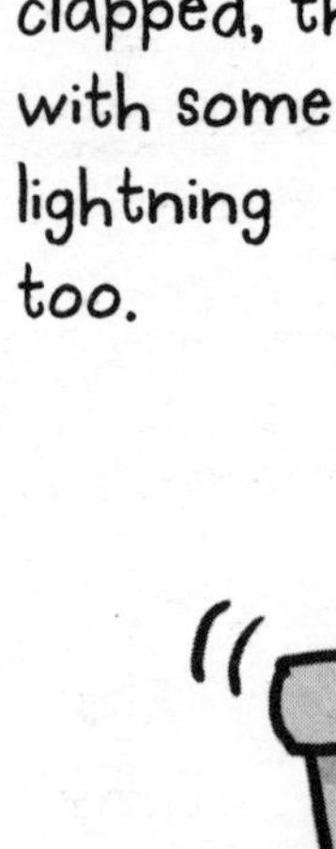

'NOT!' squawked Not Bird, waggling the donut bag in his beak, and his shiny black eyeballs peered into mine, as if he was trying to tell me something.

I scrinched my eyes shut, trying to wonder how a boring old brown paper bag filled up with a never-ending supply of donuts could possikeely help me at a time like this.

AND THEN I GOT IT.

'Oh my keelness, Not Bird! Keel idea!' I cried, and I tucked my telly belly into my trousers and straightened out my aerials, getting ready to fly up to the roof.

NEVER ENDING DONUTS

'I'm coming, Bunny!' I smiled, forward-rolling over to Not Bird and grabbing the brown paper bag, and I peered in at the pile of donuts disappearing off into the distance.

'Hold on tight, Not Bird!' I grinned, grabbing the bin and turning the bag upside down, and donut number five fell out, then donut number six, then number seven, going all the way up to infinity.

'WAAAHHH!' I screamed, as the bag shot into the air, pushed by the never-ending stream of donuts.

'Ratboy!' grinned Twoface three milliseconds later, as I let go of the bag and jumped on to the roof with Not Bird and my bin, a tower of multicoloured donuts shooting past us towards the moon.

He pulled a giant chip out of the giant chip packet and threw it over to me. 'Whack the scorpion over the head with it!' he shouted, whacking the scorpion over the head with his one.

'OWWW!' boomed Mr X's voice, and I peered through the V-shaped window on the front of his scorpion.

A shadowy figure standing at a control desk pressed a button, and a bright green laser shot out the end of the scorpion's tail.

'WAAAHHH!' I screamed, throwing my giant plastic chip, and the laser zapped it into a million normal-sized ones. 'These chips are a lot lighter than you'd imagine!' I shouted, pulling another one out of the packet, and Twoface nodded, looking over at the giant plastic cheesebleurgher.

'Are you thinking what I'm thinking?' he smiled.

'I don't know, what are you thinking?' I said, thinking maybe he was thinking we could all go for a cheesebleurgher once this was finished. Not that that was what I was thinking, seeing as I was thinking I was going to get zapped home by lightning inside my bin with Not Bird as soon as we'd saved Bunny.

'I was thinking we could use the cheesebleurgher as a giant Frisbee to throw at the scorpion!' shouted Twoface, and I nodded, even though it sounded like the ridikeelousest idea ever.

EXPLODING FRISBEE CHEESEBLEURGHER

Twoface backed towards the cheesebleurgher while I distracted Mr X with my giant chip. Splorg and Jamjar had reached the roof, and were climbing up the straw towards Bunny, which was a lot easier for Jamjar, seeing as she had five arms.

'MUCH. HEAVIER. THAN. THE. CHIPS,' wheezed Twoface, lifting the cheesebleurgher above his head and zigzagging around on the spot underneath it.

'I LAUGH IN THE FACE OF YOUR GIANT PLASTIC CHEESEBLEURGHER!' roared Mr X from inside the scorpion, his shadow pressing a button, and a bright green laser shot out of the scorpion's tail towards Twoface.

The cheesebleurgher bun exploded, firing giant plastic sesame seeds the size of Not Bird in every direction, and Twoface staggered towards the edge of the building, still carrying a giant slice of gherkin.

'Urgh, I HATE gherkins!' he wailed, one of his feet waggling over the edge.

'Twoface!' screamed Jamjar from inside the hole at the top of the straw, and I dropped my chip, leaping to grab Twoface's arm, or his leg, or one of his two noses.

'By the power of keelness!' I shouted, grabbing one of the little wings sticking out of his hood, and the gherkin fell through the air, crashing on to DOREEN XL97-220 below.

'BEHIND YOU, RATBOY!' cried Splorg, and I twizzled my head round to see the window on the front of the scorpion, smashed to pieces by a Not-Bird-sized sesame seed.

Inside, growling at me, was Mr X.

OPERATION GIANT BUBBLEGUM BALLOON

'YOU BROKE MY SCORPION'S WINDOW!' boomed Mr X, even though it was one of the giant plastic sesame seeds that'd broken it, not me.

The scorpion stomped towards me, snapping its giant claws, and I looked around for another giant plastic chip to whack it with. 'Catch!' shouted Twoface, throwing me the last chip, and I caught it with one hand, which is the sort of keel thing I do.

AND THAT WAS WHEN I SPOTTED THE COILY METAL ARM OUT OF THE CORNER OF MY EYE.

'WAAAHHH! IT'S MAVIS 3000!' I cried, as MAVIS 3000 clawed her way on to the roof. 'She must have clambered up the side of the building with her claws!' I shouted, explaining everything to the gang in case they didn't understand what was going on.

Not Bird zoomed through the air as lightning zigzagged all around us, the sky clapping him like HE was the superhero, not me or Twoface.

'NOT!' he screeched, pecking at MAVIS 3000's bum, even though he should've known that didn't do anything by now, seeing as he'd already tried it on DOREEN XL97-220.

MAVIS 3000 stood up and swatted Not Bird away while unwrapping a tiny little rectangle packet.

Inside was a cube of pink bubblegum, which she popped into her mouth. 'OPERATION GIANT BUBBLEGUM BALLOON!' she bleeped, blowing a familikeels-looking pink bubble.

She chomped her teeth down and the bubble floated out of her mouth, towards my shiny full-stop nose.

'Operation Don't Get Swallowed Whole By Another Giant Bubblegum Balloon!' I shouted, waving my plastic chip, and the bubble wafted over to Twoface, swallowing him up whole instead.

'WAAAAHHH!' he screamed, lifting off the roof floor inside the giant pink bubble.

'HA HA HA HA HA HA HA HA!' boomed Mr X, as Twoface floated off towards the moon. He waggled his joystick, and the scorpion turned to face Bunny, Jamjar and Splorg, who were now all sitting inside the hole at the top of the giant plastic straw. 'NO MORE MR NICE GUY!' he boomed, not that he'd been being very nice so far, and he pressed his button again.

The scorpion's tail whipped into the air, and a bright green laser shot out of it, splicing the straw in half.

'YIPPEE!' bleeped MAVIS 3000, who was clip-clopping towards me, not that I was taking any notice – I was too worried about Bunny, Jamjar and Splorg.

'HELLLPPP!' they screamed, as the straw toppled to the roof floor, and they rolled onto the ground like three giant drops of extra fizzy cola.

The scorpion stepped forwards, placing its giant metal foot on Bunny's fat belly, just enough so she couldn't move. 'Get off of her!' screamed Jamjar, bashing the scorpion's ankle with her five arms, while Splorg fished around in Bunny's apron pocket like he was looking for something.

'Got it,' he said, whipping out Bunny's soggy flannel and patting her on the forehead with it.

'NOT!' screeched Not Bird, zooming towards the scorpion's bum like a giant plastic sesame seed and pecking at it with his little beak. MAVIS 3000 carried on clip-clopping towards me, her coily metal arms stretched out in front of her.

I looked over at my bin where I'd parked it on the other side of the roof, and a lightning bolt exploded next to it. The bin shot up in the air, did a loop-the-loop, and crash-landed on the roof's edge, swaying up and down like a seesaw. 'MY BIN!' I screamed, dropping my giant plastic chip and running towards it.

The scorpion's claws clamped shut and jaggedy triangles popped out of their edges, transforming them into rotating saws.

'DON'T WORRY, THIS WON'T HURT A BIT!' boomed Mr X, as the spinning metal teeth centimetred towards Bunny's ten waggling arms, and another bolt of lightning zigzagged through the sky, just in case the whole thing wasn't scary-looking enough already.

GLADYS 5000

'HOO HOO HA HA HAAA!' laughed Mr X, not that he sounded all that happy. 'MY CREATION IS ALMOST COMPLETE!' he roared, as I ran towards my bin.

I skidded to a stop by the bin and dragged it back on to the roof, standing it up straight and jumping in.

'Why are you doing this to me?!' screamed Bunny, as the saws spun towards her fifty fingers.

'Yeah Mr X, why can't you just leave everyone alone!?' shouted Splorg, and I peered out of my bin and through a gap in the scorpion's broken window, spotting Dr Smell's nose, Delores's ears, and Dindle Frogshnoff's eyes, all bobbing around inside an enormous fish tank.

'The body parts!' I gasped. 'They're all here!'

'RATBOY ON TOAST!' bleeped MAVIS 3000, who'd twizzled round and started clip-clopping after me in the opposite direction, but I just ignored her and carried on peering through the broken window.

Next to the tank floated a see-through screen with a picture of the strangest-looking creature I'd ever seen on it. And I'd seen a lot of strange-looking creatures recently.

It had Dr Smell's nose, and Delores's ears. It had thirteen eyes, which I guessed must be Dindle Frogshnoff's ones, and sticking out of its body, which looked like it was made out of a bit of old robot granny, were Bunny's ten arms. Next to the picture, in scary-looking capital letters, were the words 'GLADYS 5000'.

Mr X peered down at Bunny and tilted his eyebrows into their scary positions. 'SNIP SNIP!' he roared, as Twoface floated past the window of the scorpion, inside his giant pink bubble. 'Don't worry gang, Twoface is back!' he boomed, doing his superhero grin.

'Twoface!' I shouted, pointing at the picture of GLADYS 5000, and he floated round to look at it, then turned to me.

'What? I don't get it!' he said, floating upside down, his two faces turning red.

'Don't you see what's happening here?' I cried, pointing at the picture. MAVIS 3000 had almost reached me, but I reckoned I had time to say one more sentence first. 'Mr X is building a brand-new, super-duper-keel, undefeatable-can't-be-beatable robot granny out of all the stolen body parts!' I said, and Twoface gasped.

'Ohh! I see what's going on here!' said Twoface, clicking his fingers inside his bubble. 'Mr X is building a new robot granny out of all the stolen body parts!' he smiled, copying exactly what I'd just said.

SORRY MAVIS

MAVIS 3000 stopped clip-clopping towards me and turned to look up at Mr X, her metal eyebrows tilting into their sad positions. 'IS THIS TRUE, MR X?' she bleeped, as a lightning bolt exploded two millimetres from my bin.

'SORRY MAVIS 3000, BUSINESS IS BUSINESS!' boomed Mr X, speeding up the spinning saws, and Bunny screamed. He pushed his joystick forwards, and I looked around for Not Bird, seeing as there was no way I was going to get zapped home inside my bin without him.

'Not Bird!' I cried, spotting him pecking at the giant plastic chip I'd just dropped. 'There's no time for snacks – get the keelness over here NOW!'

Not Bird looked up at me, then over at Bunny, who was still screaming. Jamjar was tapping her Triangulator and pointing it at Mr X's scorpion, her four spare arms flailing at the spinning saws. Splorg carried on patting Bunny's forehead with the soggy flannel.

'NOT!' screeched Not Bird, grabbing the plastic chip in his little beak and trying to lift it.

'What the unkeelness are you doing!?' I screamed, as a lightning bolt zapped past my full-stop nose, almost slicing it off. I jumped out of the bin and forward-rolled across the roof, scooped up Not Bird, and was just about to start running back to my bin when a raindrop tapped against my scuba mask and zigzagged down it like a tear.

I thought back to that Saturday night in my living room at home, when the window had been crying, and how I'd forward-rolled across the carpet with a tissue to cheer it up – because I was a superhero, and that's what superheroes do.

I looked down at the plastic chip Not Bird had been trying to pick up. 'BY THE POWER OF KEELNESS!' I boomed, picking it up and swiping it at the scorpion's legs.

'NOOO!' roared Mr X, as scorpion leg number one crashed into scorpion leg number two, which crashed into scorpion leg number three, going all the way up until the scorpion tipped sideways, its fish tank smashing and the stolen body parts pouring all over MAVIS 3000.

'NIGHT NIGHT,' warble-bleeped MAVIS 3000, her red traffic-light eyes popping and smoke billowing out of her ears.

'Quick, get the body parts!' cried Splorg, helping Bunny to her feet, and him, Bunny and Jamjar scrabbled around picking them all up, which didn't take long seeing as they had seventeen arms between them.

'I'LL GET YOU FOR THIS!' boomed Mr X, waggling his joystick, and the scorpion leaned backwards, teetering on the edge of the building.

'NOT!' screeched Not Bird, tapping the scorpion's forehead with his beak, and it slipped off the roof and fell into the air.

PHEW, SORT OF

I forward-rolled over to the edge of the building and stared down at the pavement. 'Phew, that was close!' I smiled. The giant metal scorpion had crashed to the ground and was lying next to DOREEN XL97-220, its green eyes fading to black.

'My superhero!' cried Bunny, managing to give me a cuddle even though she was still holding all the stolen body parts, and I high-fived Splorg, then Jamjar, giving her a high-twenty-five seeing as she had five hands, and I was in a good mood.

NOT THAT MY GOOD MOOD WAS GOING TO LAST FOR LONG.

I looked up in the sky, smiling, and immediately stopped smiling. The storm cloud had floated off into the distance, just like the one on the moon had the day before.

'MY LIGHTNING! HOW AM I GOING TO GET HOME NOW?!' I screamed, wondering how long it'd be until the next storm.

Jamjar tapped her fingers on the Triangulator and looked up too. 'Hmmm, looks like there's a fluctuation in the biometric quadrant that's destabilising the entire jet stream for the northern sector.'

'AND . . . ?' I cried, pushing my scuba mask on to my forehead.

'Could be another storm here within the fortnight,' she said, and I looked down at the ground.

'NOT!' screeched Not Bird, pecking at Twoface's bubble, and it popped, dropping him on to the roof next to me.

'Good work, Ratboy!' he grinned, patting me on my back, and he patted himself on his back too. 'Bunny's right – maybe you are a superhero after all!' he said, and Splorg and Jamjar nodded.

'Yeah, Ratboy!' said Splorg. 'All you need now is your superhero name!' he grinned, his dinosaur teeth glinting in the Sunkeels afternoon sun.

'Hmmm . . . a superhero name,' I said, glancing up and half-smiling again, seeing as a couple of weeks in the future didn't sound TOO bad. 'How about Colin Lamppost!' I beamed, and they all shook their heads.

Bunny ruffled my aerials with one of her spare hands, and Dr Smell's nose twitched, maybe because he'd sniffed my eight-million-year-old pants. 'I think you're more of a FUTURE RATBOY!' she smiled, and Dindle Frogshnoff's thirteen eyes all blinked in agreement.

Suddenly there was a scraping sound from the road below, and I peered down at the pavement, spotting the giant metal scorpion stumbling back on to its feet. 'FUTURE RATBOY, EH?' boomed Mr X's voice, and he smiled up at me through his broken window. 'I TOLD YOU I'D GET YOU FOR THIS!' he cackled, pressing a button.

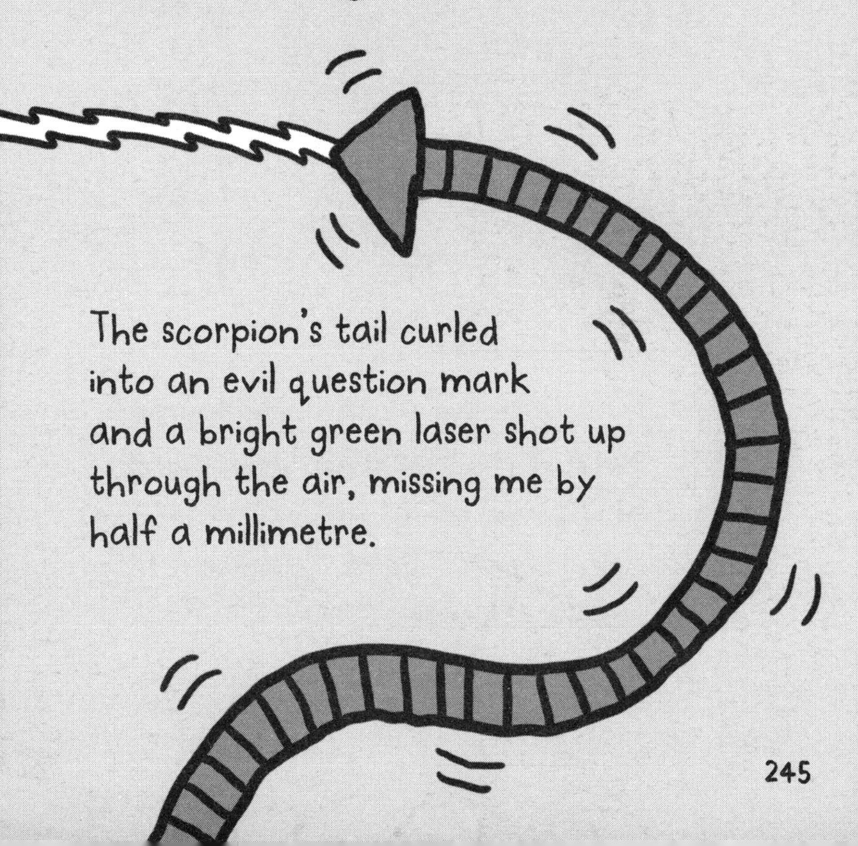

The scorpion's tail curled into an evil question mark and a bright green laser shot up through the air, missing me by half a millimetre.

'Phew, that was close!' I said in my Future Ratboy voice, turning round to see the laser zap my wheelie bin.

'NOOO!' I screamed, as the bin glowed lumo green, then fizzled into nothing. 'My bin! Now I'll never get home!' I wailed, and the scorpion clomped off down Shnozville High Street, Mr X laughing to himself.

STUCK IN THE FUTUREKEELS

Not Bird flew over and landed on my head, and Splorg put his hand on my shoulder. 'Don't worry, Future Ratboy, we'll get your bin back,' he said, looking over at Twoface.

'Yeah, piece of cake!' said Twoface, plucking a piece of plastic gherkin out of his hood, and I stared at Jamjar, who was already tapping something into her Triangulator.

'The laser seems to have discombobulated the internal metrics of your wheelie bin,' she warbled, pushing her glasses up her nose. 'I'll have to totally reconfigure the Triangulator's homing modules if we're ever going to have a chance of finding it – but I'll figure it out!' she said, as a tear zigzagged down my cheek.

Bunny gave me a cuddle and wiped my tear away with her flannel. 'Until then, looks like you're stuck with us lot!' she grinned, and I looked at her ten arms and Jamjar's five, Twoface's two faces and Splorg's one big blue one.

'I spose there's weirder people to play it keel with,' I said, and then I realised something.

'Wait a minute, if today's Sunkeels . . . doesn't that mean it's school tomorrow?' I gasped, and they all sniggered.

'Don't be silly, Future Ratboy!' said Splorg. 'There's no school here in the future!' he laughed, and my plug-tail did a wiggle.

'Now THAT'S something I could get used to!' I grinned, jumping a centimetre off the ground and shouting 'KEEL!' so loud I reckon even my mum and dad and little sister might've heard it.

THE END

"ABOUT THE AUTHOR"

Jim Smith is the keelest kids' book author in the whole world amen.

He graduated from art school with first class honours (the best you can get) and went on to create the branding for a sweet little chain of coffee shops.

He also designs cards and gifts under the name Waldo Pancake.

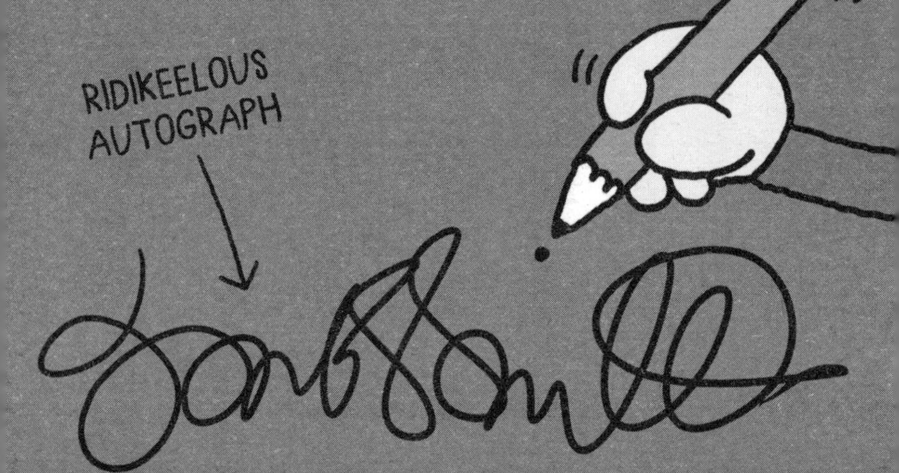

Wait a minute, where's my Edam?!
BUNNY DELI